The Sponge Who Saved CHRISTMAS

Written by Melissa Wygand • Illustrated by Fabrizio Petrossi

A GOLDEN BOOK • NEW YORK

created by

Stephen Hillenburg

randomhouse.com/kids
Educators and librarians, for a variety of teaching tools, visit RHTeachersLibrarians.com
ISBN: 978-0-307-97596-6
Printed in the United States of America
10 9 8 7 6 5 4 3 2 1

It was Christmastime in Bikini Bottom. Decorations were being hung. Gifts were being wrapped. Everyone loved the holiday season. Well, almost everyone.

Squidward didn't like Christmas.
But not because he had to work extra
shifts at the Krusty Krab.

And not because he never got any cards or gifts.

Squidward didn't like Christmas because at that time of year, SpongeBob was even happier and more annoying than usual!

SpongeBob didn't know that he was the reason Squidward was so unhappy. And seeing Squidward in such a grumpy mood just made SpongeBob want to cheer him up.

SpongeBob decided to share as much seasonal
joy with Squidward as possible. So whenever he and
Patrick had a snowball fight, they made sure to
include Squidward—whether he was ready or not.

SpongeBob and Patrick tried to lift Squidward's spirits by singing Christmas carols all day long. Everywhere Squidward went, they shared the gift of music with him. But that didn't seem to work, either.

The day before Christmas, it all became
oo much for Squidward. "I can't even hear
ny clarinet over all that caroling!"

He leaned out his window to tell SpongeBob
nd Patrick to clam up once and for all.
nstead, he got a snowball in his clarinet.

"I've had enough of this holiday!" yelled Squidward. "It's all Santa this, and presents that!

"And who does this Santa guy think he is, anyway? He's got a flying sleigh and magic reindeer? He gives you stuff for free? I'll believe it when I see it!

"If Santa's as great as everyone says he is," Squidward demanded, "then why can't he shovel my snow?"
SpongeBob didn't have an answer. He sadly walked home.

Squidward didn't hear anything from SpongeBob for the rest of the day. There were no carols, no jingling bells, and no snowball fights. As Squidward brushed his teeth, he felt quite happy.

Squidward settled into his bed, pleased at the
idea that Christmas would be over soon and things
would go back to normal. But just as he was falling
asleep, bright lights filled his room.

Squidward ran to the window. "You've got to be kidding me!" he exclaimed.

Across the way, SpongeBob's house was covered with colorful flashing and blinking lights and other Christmas decorations!

"That's it! That's the last straw!" Squidward shouted. He knew exactly what he needed to do. He marched over to SpongeBob's house.

Squidward couldn't find a way to turn off the lights. There were no plugs or switches outside. So he marched up to SpongeBob's door.

"SpongeBob!" Squidward screamed. "SpongeBob! Where are you?"

There was no answer, and after a moment, Squidward decided to go inside.

His jaw dropped. Decorations and lights filled the room from the floor to the ceiling!

"I hope SpongeBob asked Santa to pay his electric bill, heh," Squidward murmured to himself.

SpongeBob's house was so cluttered, Squidward was quickly tangled in lights and garland. "How am I ever going to find the cords in this mess?" he wondered.

After some fumbling and falling, he found the cords and unplugged the lights. Finally, everything was quiet and dark . . . but Squidward knew that wouldn't be good enough.

"SpongeBob will just plug these lights in again," Squidward
told himself. "I have to hide them until Christmas is over."
He got a bag and stuffed SpongeBob's decorations into it.

He took the stockings from the mantel . . .

. . . and the lights
from the window.

He even took the "Free Cookies" sign from Santa's plate.

But just as Squidward reached for the star on the tree, he heard a noise.

Squidward slowly turned around. There was SpongeBob, with a smile that grew bigger and bigger.

"Santa, it's really you!" SpongeBob gasped. "But why are you taking my things?"

Squidward quickly realized that SpongeBob
thought he was Santa Claus! He didn't want to
get caught taking SpongeBob's decorations,
so he played along.

"Well, I noticed that your lights weren't bright
enough," Squidward said. "So I thought I'd take
them to my workshop to get them fixed."

"That's good enough for me!" SpongeBob said. "But before you go, I have something to give you!" SpongeBob rushed to his closet and threw open the doors. He took out a box wrapped in shiny paper.

SpongeBob handed the box to Squidward. "Could you please take this present to my neighbor, Squidward Tentacles? I figured he probably didn't make your 'nice' list, being so miserable and all, but I wanted him to wake up on Christmas morning and find something under his tree."

Squidward was very surprised. He promised he would deliver the present. Then SpongeBob gave Squidward a big hug and went back to bed.

Curious, Squidward quickly tore open the wrapping paper.
Inside was a beautifully crafted clarinet case made of the
best driftwood money could buy!

Squidward suddenly felt bad. He realized why SpongeBob's house had been so quiet that day. SpongeBob had spent all that time making the perfect present for Squidward, while Squidward had been thinking how nice it was without SpongeBob around.

Then Squidward realized what Christmas was all about. It wasn't just about snowball fights, caroling, or even big flashy lights. It was also about friends, and being kind to them.

And so, one by one, Squidward returned all of
SpongeBob's lights and decorations to their proper
spots. The house was lit up once again.

When Squidward got home, he placed his clarinet in SpongeBob's handmade case—it was a perfect fit! He smiled and headed to bed.

Just when he was about to nod off, Squidward heard
noises outside his window—jingling bells and a jolly laugh.
He quickly got up to investigate. When he looked out
the window, he couldn't believe what he saw!

There in the sky was a flying sleigh being pulled by magic reindeer, and a man in a big red suit. It could only be one person: Santa Claus! Squidward heard him yell, "These cookies are fantastic!"

Squidward stood staring for a moment as the voice
faded into the night. Then he looked down at the ground.
Santa had shoveled his snow!

"It's going to be a merry Christmas after all," Squidward said.